Birds

Julie Haydon

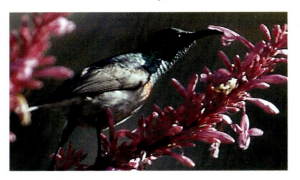

NELSON

™

THOMSON LEARNING

Australia · Canada · Mexico · Singapore · Spain · United Kingdom · United States

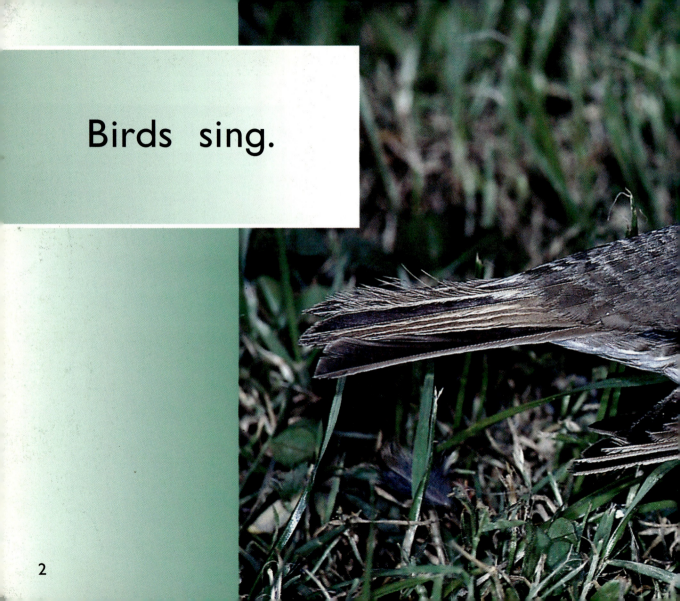

Birds sing.

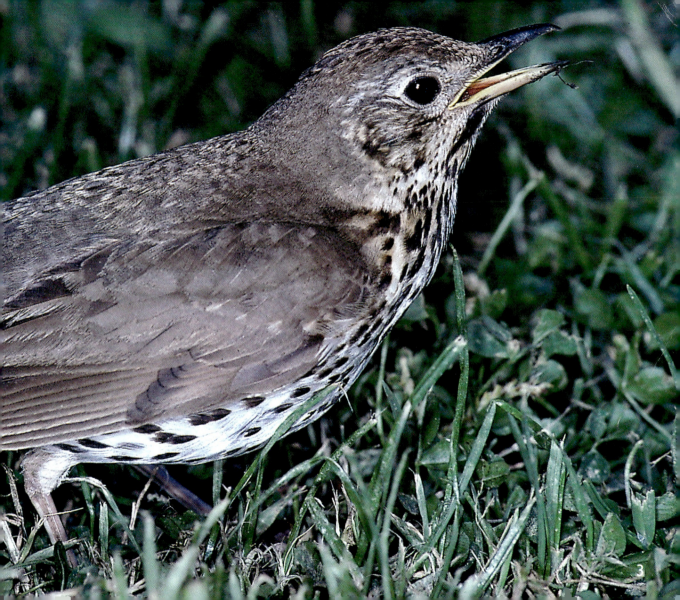

Birds eat.

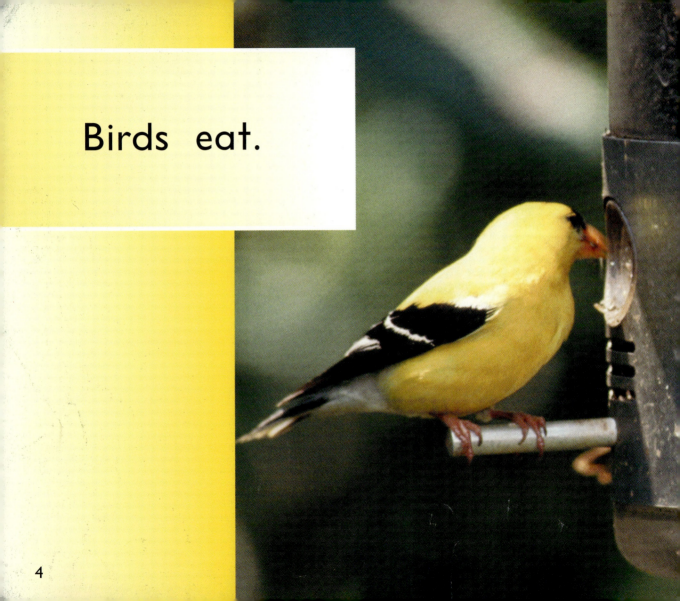

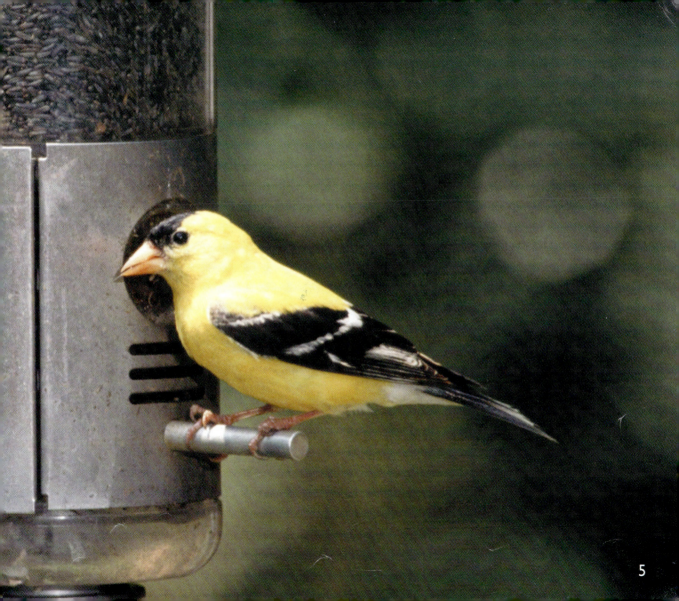

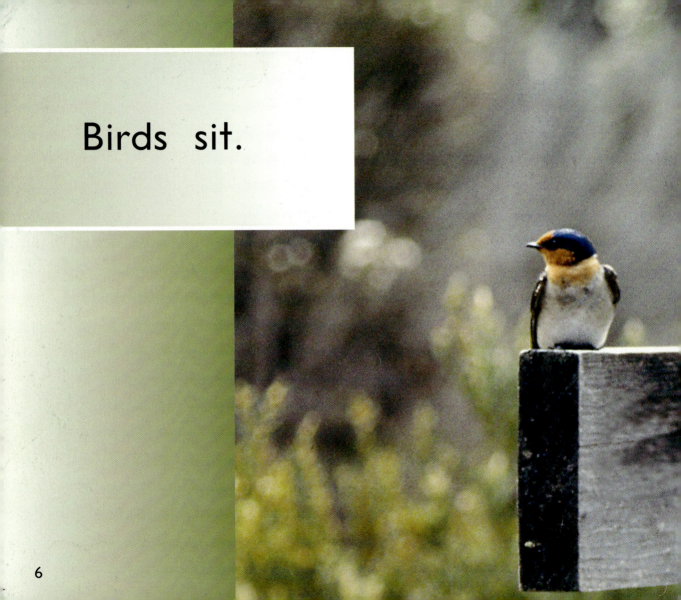

Birds sit.

6

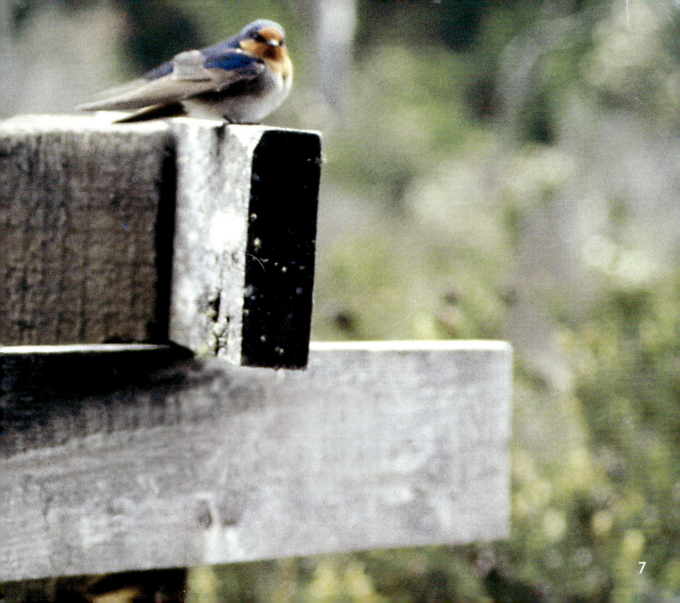

Birds drink.

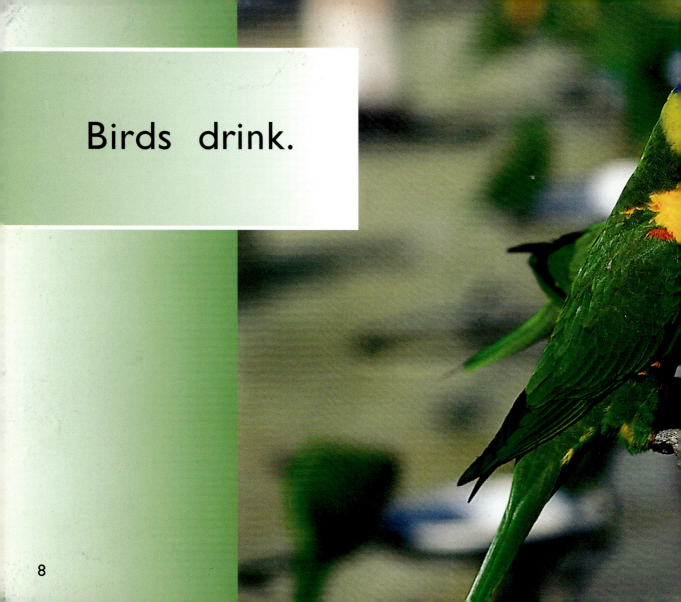

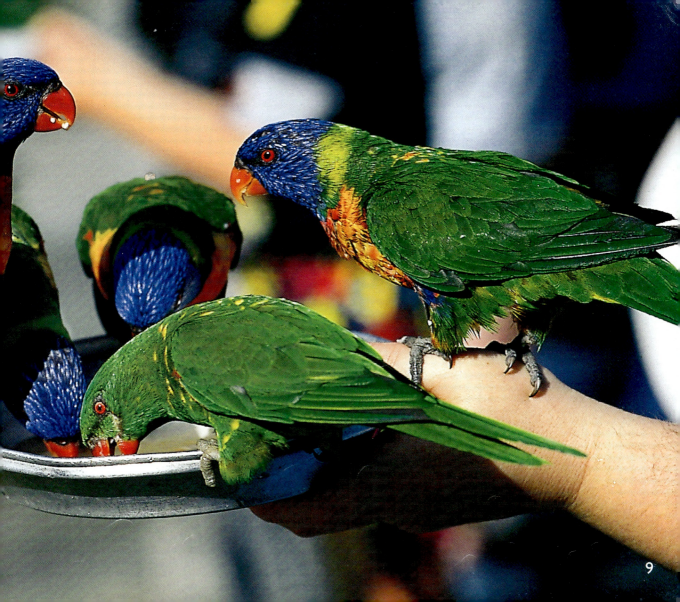

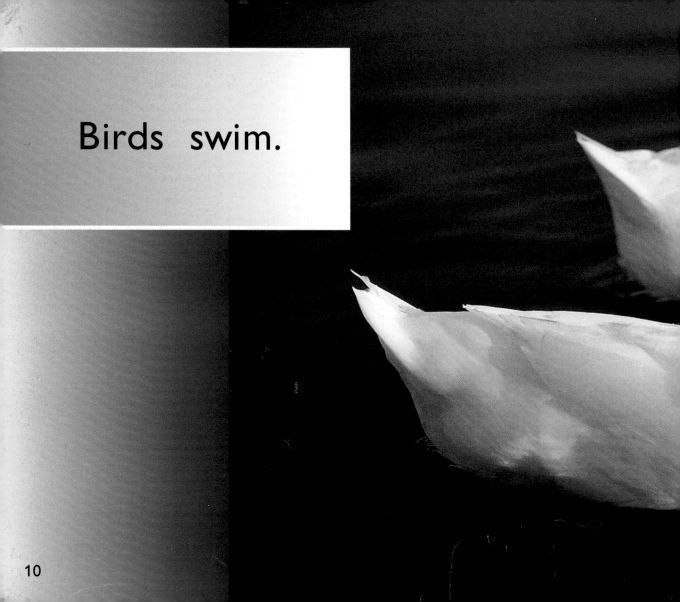

Birds swim.

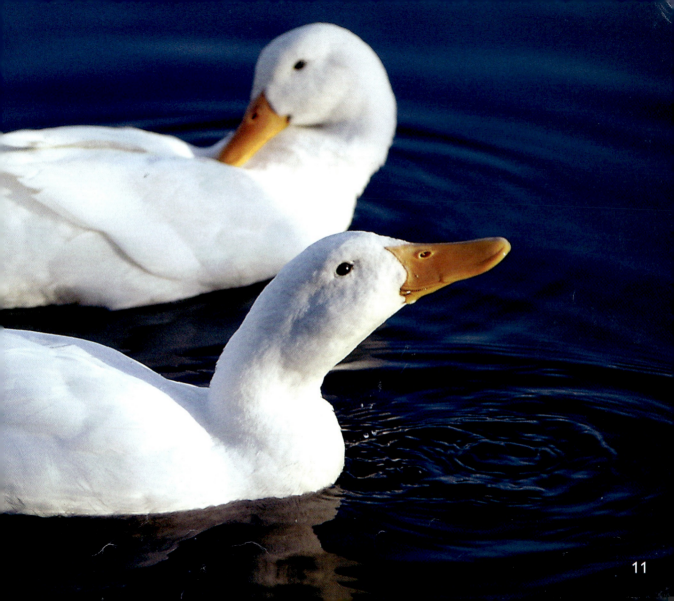

Birds fly.

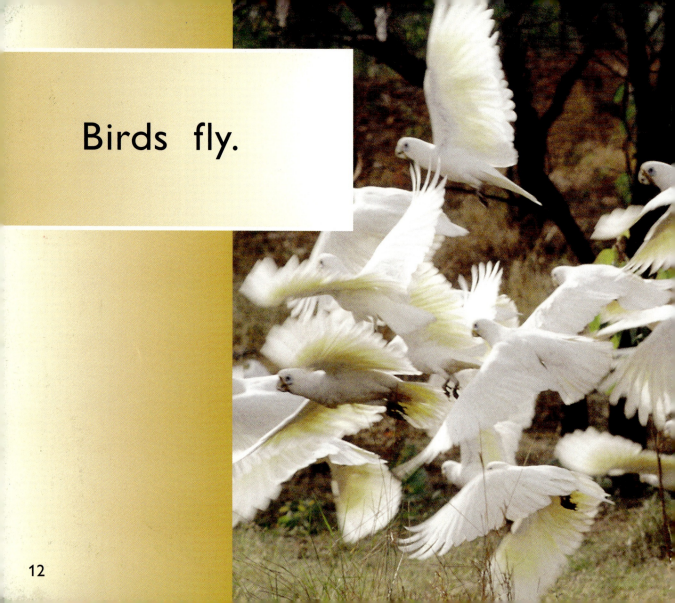

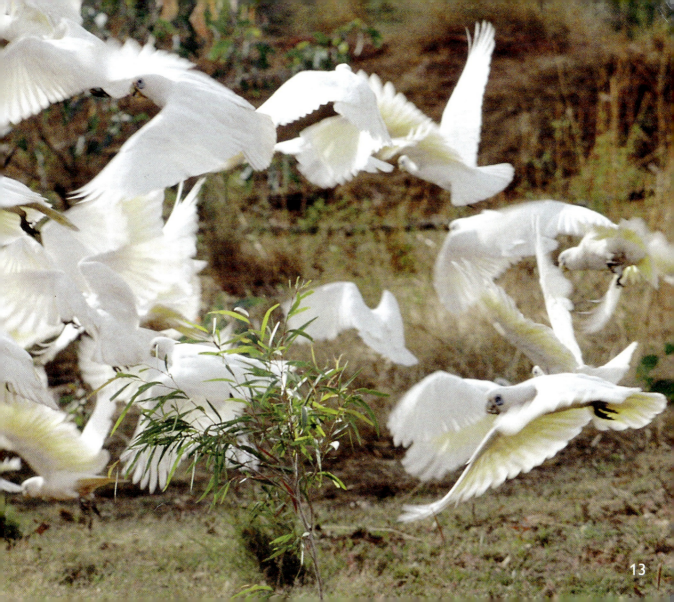

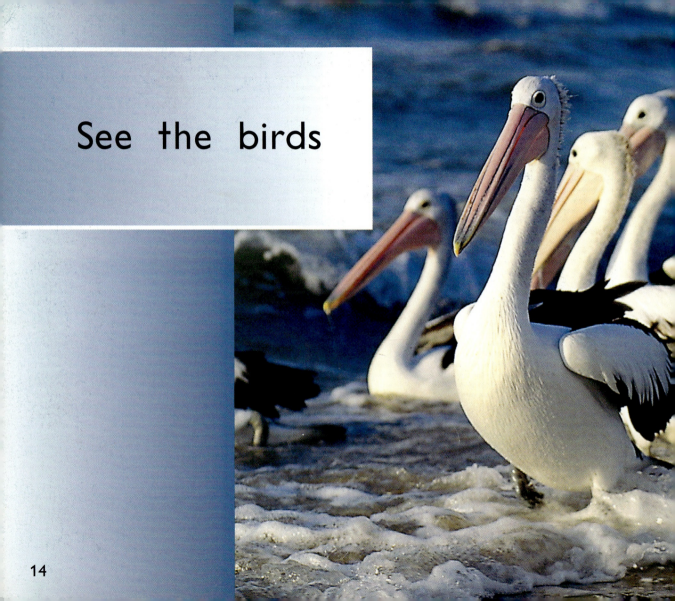

See the birds

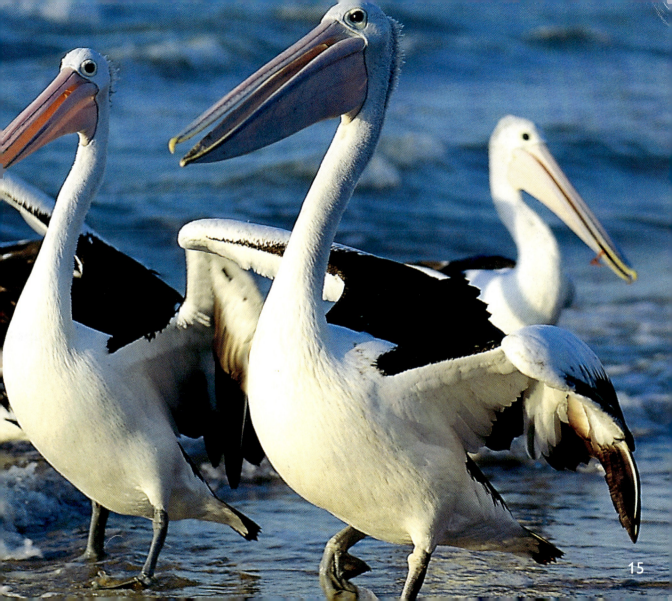

in the sky.

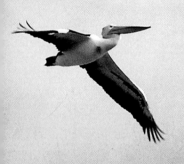
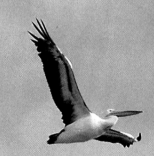
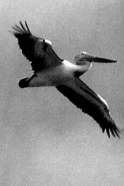